THE WAY OF LILITH

PIETRO GIORDANO

We are angels still sleeping

the heavy sleep of the flesh.

Man must awaken,

open your eyes to the truth

 if you don't want to

risk crossing life

like an unconscious brute.

Paracelsus

Prologue

To a lover of the unknown, the mysteries of alchemy, the extraordinary... Can it happen to meet a very special teacher? Perhaps yes, if the desire is so strong and intimate to activate that famous Law of Universal Resonance of which many speak.

 Let yourself be led in the intense adventure of David, thirty years old, deeply attracted by the search for something more than the scientific coldness of reality, the flow of everyday life and normal interpersonal relationships. A seemingly quiet holiday in the paradise of the Amalfi Coast gives him the encounter that will turn his life upside down forever, dragging him into an adventure that will lead him to the discovery of the most arcane mysteries of this Universe, an encounter that will give him everything that many aspirants were granted only after numerous reincarnations and long initiatory paths, and discovering secrets about himself that he could not even dream of.

The need to escape

That terrible ringing alarm clock noise!

"It's a good thing today is the last day of work before the holidays," David thought before he started getting ready to go to work. He was employed in an office in a small village of central Italy, and despite that cool September morning he was taking him to work, he was already with his head in the beautiful Amalfi Coast.

It had been a long time since he and his ex-had planned a fortnight-long love escape in the beautiful southern part of Italy, but after they had recently broken up after a long period of misunderstandings, he decided to go and take advantage of the already paid reservation, as well as the incredible period of good weather that was pampering the southern regions at that time of the year; it would have done him nothing but good. At the end of the shift, as almost every day David used to go to the running course to run a bit, he was very keen to keep fit.

 Once home, after a light dinner accompanied by a glass of wine, he loved to dedicate himself to the passion that had taken hold of him for some years: the occult, the magic and the Extraordinary, which had led him to collect an imposing themed bookshop.

Deep down he did not accept that life should stop at: work - home - work, then get married, have a family, grow old and die. This could not be the only meaning of life. Reading the saga of Castaneda, he felt an immense envy for the author, whocould learn the occult art from a powerful sorcerer like Don Juan, "maybe one day I will find my Don Juan too" he fantasized on his couch;

"he who will be able to take me by the hand into the knowledge of the Universe."

The night flew by quickly, and with a few glasses of wine of to much, that night he had strange dreams, tarot cards talking to him, strange animals never seen before, and fluctuations of his body in open spaces, "I must stop overdoing it with wine," he thought.

But the time had come to prepare to leave. His little Italian hatchback would take him to that picturesque place that until then he had only seen from online photos.

Magical sunsets and wonderful walks by the sea awaited him. The journey lasted

only a few hours, and once he passed the
pass of the Lattari Mountains that protects
the Coast, a breathtaking scenery
appeared in front of him: he had arrived!
He went to the address agreed with the
landlord, it was just as he had imagined
the house, near the sea so that every day
he could admire the purple color of the
sunset.

He found the owner of the property
waiting for him in the street, a short, bald
man in his fifties who as soon as he saw
him, in an Italian influenced by the
dialect, asked him why a handsome young
man like him was not accompanied by a
sweetheart in such a romantic place.

"What can you do," exclaimed David,
"better alone than badly accompanied", he
concluded, with the approval of the
landlord.

Having arrived at dusk, he decided not to
waste even a moment of these precious

days off and to start enjoying the place right away. He inquired about evening activities and discovered that he was spoilt for choice.

He went to one of the picturesque villages on the coast to start his evening with an aperitif, and maybe make some acquaintances.

He decided that in these days he would put aside his passion for the Extraordinary and dedicate himself to "earthly" activities.

The following day David got up just after dawn to explore the Coast in search of a beautiful beach where he would spend most of the day. He had left without organizing a precise itinerary, he wanted to explore the

place and live it day after day, with all the surprises of the case, whether good or bad.

Before anything else, a hearty breakfast was essential, for a day out he needed energy, since the next meal would be dinner. When he reached the first bar near his house he ordered a cappuccino with croissant; he could admire the enchanting poetry of the sea on the rocks from the table where he was sitting, "near the sea even the food looks better, the sea must have a power we don't yet know well" he thought.

While he was still immersed in his reflections on the positive influence of the sea on people, sat down at a table right next to his a girl. Protected by the discretion of his sunglasses, he looked deep into her pretending to look beyond her, he could deduce that she was clearly younger than he was, she must was twenty-five years old at the most, he thought that she probably must not have Italian origins.

She had red hair, light mahogany, and surprisingly green eyes, which almost penetrated the protection of her sunglasses, the sea breeze let guess the delicate scent of orange blossom she was wearing.

The girl ordered, and after a while it arrived what must have been a herbal tea or tea. David took off his glasses, and could better appreciate her disarming beauty; she was tall and slender, had barely hinted freckles and a very slight squint, small imperfections that made her a perfect creature.

"Are you from around here?"

"Huh?" David came to his senses by returning from the world of fantasy.

"No, I was asking if you're from this area." She exclaimed with an accommodating smile and opened her emerald eyes.

David couldn't believe she was talking to him, I mean, a woman starting a conversation... He'd hardly ever had that. It was usually him who broke the ice.

"Yeah, I mean, no," he said to himself, "I'm Italian, but I'm not from here.

I congratulate you, you have an impeccable Italian!"

"You talk as if you were addressing a foreigner, what makes you think I'm not Italian?" said the girl giving

him another one of her deadly smiles.

Because of his prejudice he had made a gaffe, he had to regain control and manage the situation better, but those eyes had a different light, a sun-like glow on the waves of the sea, as if he were in the presence of a force of nature.

"I'm sorry, I'm on holiday alone and you're the first person I've had a word with since I've been here, I'd almost got used to talking only to myself."

The girl stopped smiling, and almost got a serious look at him, looking for his eyes. David could almost feel himself breaking through the door of his soul.

Suddenly he came to his senses and decided to face her, finding the audacity that has always distinguished him on many occasions and he showed up:

"We haven't even introduced ourselves. My name is David!" Posing with the smile.

"My name is Angela. David is a powerful and important name, you know? The meaning of the name given to us has a great influence on our lives."

He was surprised by that answer, that girl most likely shared the same passions as him but decided not to ask her anything about it. He didn't want to rush too much and already pry into her interests, maybe later he would ask her some questions to try to figure out if that was the case. In any case, there was something strange about her, a presence that made her feel uncomfortable, he found it hard to think what he wanted to tell her.

"Even the name Angela seems to be really important and meaningful, aren't angelic figures the most beautiful thing there is?" David retorted.

She looked at him seriously again, "it depends, it might even be the perfect opposite. Maybe a fallen angel... But enough about the meaning of names, the day is wonderful for a walk, and the waterfront of this country is fantastic. Do you want to go for a walk?"

He quickly accepted the invitation and agreed with her to change the subject.

They talked together for a long time, three, maybe four hours went by and David noticed that for her young age she had a wisdom he had never seen before in anyone else and he was impressed, she was already beginning to attract him.

At one point he interrupted the walk and invited her to sit on a bench nearby.

"You know, this is the first time I find myself opening up so much to someone I've only recently met. But tell me about yourself. I'd like to know what you do in life, and where you're from."

She looked at him with an expression of pleasure, as if she'd been waiting a long time for that question.

"I was born in Italy but I don't belong anywhere. I've lived an itinerant life since I was a child, changing countries, following my father's work as a painter...

It led him to change places and lives very often. My mother unfortunately I never knew her, she suddenly abandoned my father when I was only 2 years old, without a reason, leaving him a note and an amulet recommending that he gives it to me."

She took a long pause, he understood and instinctively laid his hand on her.

" I know a little about her and I learned it from my father's stories, she was a fortune teller, but she didn't do it out of need, She said about herself that it was a vocation, a duty towards humanity; she too, like my father, was almost always on the road, and she always lived like that. The relationship between her and my father has always been a leave-and-take, but he thought that after my birth things would change. Evidently it didn't."

After an embarrassing silence he apologized, it was not his intention to recall a memory that might hurt her.

The young woman played down and smiled and told him that everything that doesn't kill us has made us stronger.

"What do you do now?"

She asked him still curious to know more about her.

"My father, with his work, has accumulated an economic fund for me which he put at my disposal at the end of my studies, so that I can use it to carry out my projects, I am his only daughter and he has focused all his attention on my future. My job is an independent researcher, I go to the sites of interest to do research on site and write texts, I currently write for 3 international newspapers quite important."

He was literally amazed. He had never met anyone with such an exciting life.

The sun was high in the beautiful picture of the Amalfi Coast, it was already noon. He invited her to lunch, she refused the invitation, she had some important visits during the day for her work but at least he managed to get the mobile number.

The initiation

David didn't want to seem nagging, after all, they'd only known each other for a day, so he decided not to call her to go out that night, maybe he'd send her a message the next day. After an afternoon of rest, sheltered from the intense heat, he decided to go out in the evening to continue the discovery of that landscape that seemed painted, poetry came out of every meter traveled on those roads. He arrived in Amalfi, and walking along the pier of the small port he stopped to contemplate the moon, which that evening was full, as huge as he could not remember. With the stars and the sea in the background it looked like heaven on earth. Walking around, he thought back to

the morning spent with that strange girl
he met in that bar near the house where
he was staying, time had passed so
quickly, his presence so strong and ...

That feeling of having already had
something to do with it. He was reminded
of some of the texts he had read about
belonging to animic families and previous
lives, "maybe we met in another life"

he thought,

"but I've certainly never seen her in this
one," he concluded. And while she was
thinking of going home she began to smell
that magnificent scent of orange blossom,
she turned around to see her, but saw no
one only a group of young people talking
animatedly and an elderly couple walking.
He thought about the

possibility that the aroma came from some
nearby lemon groves in bloom, since the

Amalfi Coast has enormous cultivations of this type of fruit trees.

When he got home he took a shower, went to the balcony of the apartment and opened a bottle of wine

bought in the market of the village, starting to relax on the sofa, watching the moonlight on the sea.

The noise of the first traffic of the day woke him up.

"what the hell, I fell asleep on the balcony!"

He cried out loud.

He took his smartphone to check the time, it was already ten o'clock! But surprisingly he saw that there was an unread message.

"I just hope you don't catch a damn thing in the cold of the night, I'll be waiting for you at the bar for breakfast!"

His heart suddenly leapt, it was Angela!
He dressed quickly, and as he descended
the stairs three steps at a time he called
her to tell he was coming.

"How did you know I was sleeping on the
balcony? You wrote it in your message."
Exclaimed David smiling after saying
hello.

"Just by looking. I was walking along the
boardwalk this morning, trying to figure
out who this strange individual was who
had clearly spent the night sleeping out on
the balcony."

David laughed to play down. He invited
her for breakfast and after he asked if she
was into esotericism, New Age or some
other kind of interest in the occult.

"I've always been interested in this kind of
study, I could even claim to be a teacher!"
She said, showing her usual destabilizing
smile.

"What do you want to know? Maybe I can share some notions with you."

"How modest!"

He exclaimed David in a joking tone.

"Look, I've studied a lot about it too, maybe I can help you back up."

"We'll see...I'll start anyway!"

The young woman answered by half-closing her big green eyes while she was

watching him. Angela then spoke to him about the power of the universal source, which she called GIEM

(Great Intelligent Energy in Motion) from which all beings can draw energy, inspiration and intelligence, "we can call it God, Allah, or as you wish, GIEM is the one who maintains the structure of the Universe and regulates its main laws. He is neither good nor bad, but like the sign of the Tao, he maintains the balance of existence with the two forces: black and white, yin and yang, good and evil. She went on to say that the enormous power when attuned to our inner world can be conveyed and used to do incredible things, and people and other beings in the Universe at an advanced state already succeed.

"Unfortunately, access to this enormous power of GIEM is possible on both the dark and the light side, and the human being is one of the few creatures who can choose where and how to convey this power. Like the tarot card of the Wizard, the human being is the conductor of energy, and it is in his power to give it a polarity.

The girl talked about techniques she had never heard of before, and listed spiritual disciplines that David had not found in any book of those he had consulted, and had read quite a few. He listened to her without interrupting for hours, he was astonished. Angela spoke with such conviction that she seemed almost certain. In any case, he understood that he had a deep knowledge of the occult texts, perhaps because of the work she did, she had the opportunity to consult material that was not distributed in normal bookstores, David thought to himself.

"Okay I admit it, the GIEM story is great, and I think you really know more about it than I do. Don't you have any lyrics you could lend me? Maybe I'll look into it on these afternoons where I'm locked indoors because of the heat, then of course I'll give it back to you before I leave."

Angela got up from the chair at the bar, "I can do much more for you, follow me to my house!"

The two young arrived in front of an old building with a huge door. After a few flights of stairs they arrived at her house; it was a very large, clean and tidy apartment furnished in solid wood everywhere. David could admire on his right a bookcase containing volumes that seemed to be very old, and hanging on the walls,

relics and exotic trinkets from who knows where. Angela took a leather parchment from a desk drawer which, at first sight, must have been of great value.

"Here, study this." She said resolutely.

David unrolled it carefully, there were a multitude of strange, indecipherable symbols on it that he had never seen anywhere.

Thank you for your help, but I really don't think I can study anything from this parchment, I haven't the faintest idea what it says!" He answered with a smile.

"In fact," she said, "you don't have to study anything. You just have to observe. The symbols are twenty-seven like the days it takes the moon to make a complete revolution around the Earth, every day you will observe one for at least an hour, seriously, just like a solemn ritual for all intents and purposes. The Power soaked in these signs will unlock access to your true self, thus erasing all your limiting thought patterns and staying in the present moment without being a victim of negative emotions. After the ritual you can begin true access to all the information and knowledge you are allowed on this dimensional plane without your

ego and its fears interfering. A Short Way for all intents and purposes."

David knew what she was referring to. Many call it Centering, or the realization of the Self, but he also knew that the Self-actualization and thought control practices of one's own mind are studies that take years to bear fruit. He didn't believe them there and then. She thought it was some fake ritual sold to her by some self-

styled magician on one of her trips, which Angela had believed and was proposing to him at the time.

But suddenly she grabbed him by the arm and got close to him, almost eyes in his eyes, so that he could feel again that intoxicating fragrance of orange blossom.

"Believe me, try it. Don't study all those texts where it's explained how not to be prejudiced if you don't put them into practice."

He nodded trying to give her the best possible expression of conviction, and after a moment of glances, he decided to change the subject:

"Thank you very much, I'll be working on the artifact you lent me as early as tomorrow. Since I'm also on vacation, how would you like to go dancing together tonight? Of course, if you're not in a relationship or dating. I don't want to make trouble for you."

She didn't hesitate,

"No, I'm not seeing anyone and I have the night off. We can go."

They made a date for the evening, then said goodbye. She gave him a kiss on one cheek for the first time, recommending once again that he follows the prescriptions regarding the parchment, and as he left he took the scent of her with him as a reminder.

David showed up at Angela's house at the agreed time. When he honked the horn, she left the door, right on time. He passed in front of the car headlights before getting into the car and David noticed that she was wearing a wraparound dress that highlighted the shape of the girl, her legs left him amazed. Up to that moment he had always met her dressed in comfortable linen or cotton overalls, he did not expect that statuesque physique.

He got into the car, greeted each other and set off on the night of the Amalfi Coast embroidered with sea and stars. When they reached the restaurant they went in and ordered a drink.

"How much longer do you plan to stay here on the Amalfi Coast? He asked, curious to know more about the girl's business plans.

"I don't know, I just finished the article on the Coast that I promised a publisher, now I'm going to enjoy this

paradise for a while, and maybe then I'll go to Egypt. I'd like to do something about the pyramids."

He looked at her with some disappointment, he would have liked her still working in Italy, maybe not to get lost.

She drank her mojito almost in one breath, he did the same with his black russian. They ordered drinks again.

"One day I'll teach you how the Egyptian people were light years ahead of today's technology, and how they were channeling GIEM's energy," she said while she was sipping her mojito this time more calmly.

He thought that alcohol was starting to have an effect on her but decided to take an active part in the speech.

"What certainty do we have about what you're saying? Have you read anything about it?"

"I haven't read anything about it. Simply, I was there." She answered him smiling with her eyes.

David imagined that she was alluding to reincarnation, thought that perhaps in the past the girl had undergone some regressive hypnosis to come to such statements.

"And for what reason did they lose this power?" He asked skeptical, but still intrigued.

"The reason is the same as the loss of contact with GIEM for many other men and peoples of power over millennia. Using the Energy for dark purposes without redemption ultimately destroys oneself. Everything is related, the Universe is like a mirror, sooner or later what you do comes back, whether it is a positive or

negative action".

David, though interested, suddenly closed that conversation by inviting her to dance, thought he would pick it up the next day. He remembered the promise he made to himself not to let himself be absorbed by the interests of the Extraordinary even on vacation. The young woman accepted and they threw themselves on the dance floor of the club. Just at that moment a slow song started, the DJ invited all the couples to squeeze together and enjoy that dance. David had drunk a lot, and thanks to the alcohol he felt he was proposing himself, this girl a bit strange but so cultured had taken him. He tried with his hands on her hips to dance together. The girl didn't run away. While they were dancing, David jumped up and tried to kiss her

quickly. The girl gently pushed himself away.

"David, you're drunk, no."

He whispered in her ear.

"I'm afraid I'm going to be sick." He stammered with the typical nauseous expression. He left her quickly and went to the bathroom. He locked himself in the toilet, and from there it was a big mess. People all around, auto ambulance, red and blue lights, and then the blackout. She woke up in the morning in her bed,

with a crazy headache. On the bedside table was a box of aspirin, and the parchment that Angela had given him the day before. He snapped to get his Smartphone, where he found a voice message from Angela. The

girl explained to him that he had been sick from drinking too much, but the ambulance nurses called by the club manager did not consider hospitalization necessary.

"I've arranged to call a taxi, and walk you up to the bedroom. The driver was very kind and helped me. I took the keys out of your pocket to open the door."

The girl added that she'd be out of the house for a few days and would be in touch as soon as she got back.

David had a fit of rage with himself. He had to keep his wits about him that night and try to win her over.

Instead, he'd had too much to drink and missed the precious opportunity like a fool. During the girl's two days away, he decided he would devote himself to the sea. A few swims in that beautiful sea and a bit of sunshine would have done nothing but good. In the afternoon, in the hottest hours he decided to dedicate himself to the practice suggested by Angela, he had already done some absurd things because of his interest in the world of the occult, and already for some time he had decided not to believe in those imaginary miraculous courses or spells that make the "leap", in any case he decreed that this would be the last time he spent his time on this kind of method that they knew of charlatan. He decided to do it with the utmost seriousness, if nothing else, for that girl who had taken care of him that damn evening, when she could have left him at the ambulance, they had only known each other for a few days, she owed him nothing. At the appointed time, he took the parchment and intensely observed its symbol, following the order that Angela had illustrated to him. He noticed that after a while the symbol seemed to shine slightly,

"it will be a natural reaction of the eyes, perhaps because of too much concentration."

he thought. The night before the girl returned, he went to bed very agitated. He had missed her so much in the days without her, besides the fact that he was now falling in love with her, he missed their speeches, her theses and visions.

He didn't understand if she was a little crazy, or if she was really facing some kind of witch or something. After hours he managed to reconcile his sleep, that night he had an absurd dream, he was faced with what looked like a temple immersed in a scenario that must have been the Middle East, and it didn't look like the historical period they were living in. There was not a living soul around. Something was pushing him in. He found there a huge hall, in the distance a throne raised above the floor. All around, people bowed, motionless, all dressed in the same habit. Perhaps followers of some fraternity. He looked up and couldn't believe what he saw! It was Angela, wrapped in a long green dress, which fell tightly onto her forms, letting them glimpse, highlighting her marble body. He couldn't speak, he was paralyzed.

She slowly descended barefoot from the throne and approached him. He wanted to run away but couldn't move, suddenly she caught up with him. It was only then that David could speak, and he asked who he was.

He answered in a surreal voice, not the usual tone he remembered her.

"Read the Kabbalah and you'll find out. I can't tell you my name. Know that wherever you go, if you look for me, I will be with you."

He woke up in a bath of sweat and terror. He thought that he had let himself be influenced a little bit by this girl and after having calmed down he decided to take a relaxing walk and enjoy a coffee in front of that heavenly scenery. After all, by now, the holiday was coming to an end and he wanted to take advantage until the last minute of that stay. He arrived in front of the bar where they had met, and decided to stop there.

He put his number on the phone but all the rings went blank. Maybe she was busy, or maybe after the disaster that night at the club she didn't want to see him anymore. He would have tried to find her againin the evening, if she hadn't answered, surely she had lost interest in him.

Liberation

The evening arrived inexorably with no sign of the girl's life. Just when David was facing a sunset that could not be described in words, he was putting the phone in his pocket, now resigned, the sound of a message made him jerk. It was her!

"I'm not going back to the Coast for now, unforeseen commitments unfortunately call me elsewhere. As soon as I can free myself, I'll look for you. See you anon!"

The message left him full of bitterness, he didn't expect them to suddenly separate like that. After all, he hoped to be able to continue dating her, as well as to learn new things about their common interests, he hoped above all that before he left he would have another chance to try to win her over, to show that he too could give her so much.

He said, "All right, update me when you can."

It was already time to go back in. It had certainly been the most incredible vacation he had ever had, he had seen breathtaking scenery, a beautiful sea, and what's more, he had gained two kilos because of the delicious food. A magical place that had given him the most interesting encounter of his life, and even though they would probably never see each other again, he decided to continue with rigor the ritual that Angela had given him, she wanted him to do it and did not want to disappoint her again.

By now the routine was resumed, the journey from office to home to office, the shopping, a few beers in the evenings with friends and then the bills to pay... The only thing that still kept him tied to the memory of her and that paradise on earth was the ritual that was now coming to an end. There was only one day left and only one symbol to observe. He almost regretted having completed the parchment, every time he took it to do the exercise, he would linger ten minutes to recall the memory of her, with her perfume that he

would have recognized among a thousand, that smile that lost him, her wonderful freckles. He had never heard from her again and by now, he was almost convinced that he would never do it again. That girl had a crazy life, she was free as the wind and did what she wanted. At the end of the day, what real interest could

someone like him arouse in her.

It was time for the ritual. He took the parchment and rested it carefully on his desk table, relaxed to free his mind trying not to have thoughts that hindered his concentration and began to observe the last symbol with the utmost concentration.

The alarm clock set to mark the time of exercise rang, got up from the chair and rested the parchment.

"The Moon's revolution is complete, the veil has fallen."

What was that voice in his head? Who had spoken? He didn't know, but in a moment he realized that everything had changed.

"It's not possible, I don't believe it! But this is a miracle!"

He auto observed himself and immediately noticed a profound change in his mind. A lucidity and an ability to observe without judgment never had before. Control of his thoughts and emotions was now easy, as if he had done decades of studying mind control and meditation. An immense peace pervaded him and all the fears he remembered had lost all meaning to exist. The ego he had built since he was born fell into a thousand pieces and it was like a return to life for him.

He needed to contact Angela immediately, he wanted to know more about that parchment, what was that ritual that had so radically altered the structure of his brain and made him make that evolutionary leap in such a short time? He had witnessed the Extraordinary for the first time in his life, an event that no

scientific basis could explain. He couldn't divulge that event to anyone! With his new lucidity he now knew

the nature of the human being, no one would believe him and they would take him for a fool.

He immediately took his Smartphone and tried to call her. No way, the number was nonexistent. He was not pervaded by dismay, negative emotions and anxiety no longer touched him, he was in the here and now and had full control of his mind. He stopped to think, he only had one chance! He left for the Amalfi Coast to see if she had returned to the house he had taken for her stay there. If he hadn't found her then he would have resigned himself. Thanks to the new awareness he had acquired with the parchment, he knew that once he had done all he could, he could not change that event, and from then on he would have to grow up on his own. Immediately at work he asked for permission, it would not have been a few hours by car to separate him from the possibility of finding his mentor and great passion. He packed a light luggage, a few clothes to stay out just a few days.

The snake biting its own tail

After a few hours of sleep, which was essential to gain some clarity in driving, David was already on his way to the beautiful southern town. While he was driving he was still reflecting on what had happened.

Who had written that parchment? It must have ben a very powerful magician, perhaps someone who, as Angela explained to him one day, had managed to channel and use the enormous power emanating from GIEM. He

thought of all the texts he had studied, some of them contained information to create powerful amulets that served as protection from bad influences or to give as a gift to get attention from your loved one. In short, you could give power to objects that served a specific purpose. David had always been skeptical about these practices, also because he had never met someone capable of so much in his life, and his vision

was a bit that of St. Thomas, if I don't see I don't think so.

"Angela for the kind of life she was leading must have been in contact with a powerful initiate, who left him, that written ritual."

He thought while he was already close to the goal, maybe she was herself an adept of some powerful sect, in which some Tradition of Power was transmitted.

He arrived at destination below noon, appreciating the wonderful mild climate that the Coast was able to offer despite the late October. The ritual of the parchment

50

unlocked various qualities in David, which he discovered as time went by. Now even the perception of beauty was markedly more marked, capturing all

the wonder of creation with an intensity he had never experienced before. He noticed the beauty of a flower, the pleasure of the breeze from the sea, the harmonious flight of the seagulls.

He parked his car near the girl's house, arrived at the door and tried to knock on the intercom but had no answer. He tried to turn the knob that opened the door, it was open! He decided to dare, opened it and entered slowly, calling out the girl's name. There was no answer. Unfortunately he had to see that the furniture had been removed, all the ancient ornaments and the finds were gone. She was clearly definitively gone.

"My good fortune is that I can now master my emotions in a totally different way, I don't know how I would have managed the disappointment until a few days ago."

He reflected as he closed the door to the apartment. As he walked towards the car he thought that this experience was over, it had happened that a Great Soul had passed through his life and helped him to accelerate to a new plane, now he would continue on his own. She had given him a gift that was priceless, he had to do his best to continue the evolution.

"By now I have covered almost 500 kilometers, and I have another day's stop from work. Even if she's gone, I'll get a room and sleep here tonight, I'll have enjoyed another day in this paradise."

Concluded between David and himself. He dined beautifully in a small restaurant by the sea, drank a good local wine and decided to take a walk to the harbor before returning home. His luck ran out, even though it was late October, it was a wonderful evening, and the night was a dreamy starry sky. Arrived at the end ofthe port, he decided to climb the rocks, he wanted to get away from the lights of the port to enjoy the spectacle of the night.

His heart was beating fast with emotion, and he let his heart be moved, he didn't want to control himself in front of so much beauty.

"David."

He turned around, it was her.

"I saw you coming out of the restaurant, I came back to give the keys to my former apartment and I followed you here."

He couldn't hold back, he snapped at her and hugged her hard, then kissed her hard. This time, she didn't wander off. They made love there, on the rocks, with the passion and passion of two people who had been searching for a millennium. He had made love many times, but with her he had the feeling he was making love for the first time.

Her skin, her lips, everything seemed new, and it was beautiful.

They stayed there embraced and slept until dawn, with the sound of the sea to keep him company. At the first light of the sun she woke him with a caress and a kiss, as soon as he was present and recovered, Angela asked him to kneel down, close his eyes and have all his attention. She was more serious than ever, and she aroused respect. He obeyed.

The girl solemnly began to speak.

"This is the sacred love made with the first Teacher, I now begin to understand. You have eaten the fruit from the tree of knowledge, with my sign you are reborn without contamination and will be given to learn the Knowledge."

She paused briefly, then continued, this time in her usual tone of voice, relaxed and accommodating.

The formula is over, know that I have been watching you for many lifetimes, and I have loved your primordial soul qualities since your first times on this Earth, you were looking for the wisdom to free yourself, and now it was time. From now on, don't look for me anymore, our planes of existence are too far apart and I could destroy you even without wanting to."

She made marks with her fingers on his face, then silence around him.

David remained in the position requested by Angela for a few minutes, apart from the sound of the sea breaking on the rocks and the screams of the seagulls he could not hear any other sound.

He decided to open his eyes, she was no longer there.

On the way home, David thought about what had happened to him. The scenes flowed before his eyes like a movie, now he knew there were souls extremely evolved, and he had known one, the skepticism he had fallen like shattered glass.

 The mind was already processing thoughts of lack and nostalgia, but he blocked them immediately.

Angela was right, the difference between them was remarkable, a stable relationship with a woman like that could not be possible, "she and I are like a glass and a pool," he thought, "how much water can a pool give a glass? I will accept the current state of things, making a promise to myself: one day I will be a pool too, and we will meet again in some other life". Though inside he was certain that she would cherish his memory too.

Months went by, colleagues and friends realized that David was different, with a new light in his eyes, he was never irritated, he was always positive and had a much more marked concentration and intelligence.

Always ready to help, but not for this fool, he recognized a trick or a sly one a kilometer away, keeping away from it.

Everyone attributed David's change to the holiday and many asked him what he had done on the Amalfi Coast to return to that state of constant calm and happiness. The answer was always the same:

"Whatever you want, it will be the air of
that paradise that did me good".

He never told anyone about the meeting
he had, that holiday was the most precious
thing that had ever happened to him in
this life, and that secret kept him jealously
inside.

Become a swimming pool

Some time had passed since those fateful words that Angela uttered before telling him not to look for her anymore, and from time to time they still echoed in his head. In hindsight he thought it over, it didn't have to mean goodbye. They were just too far away, at the moment the knowledge of that mysterious emerald-

eyed creature would destroy him, his mind would not be able to stand all the secrets and teachings that someone like her could give him. One thought wouldn't let him go: if he had been able to grow on the soul plane, she would most likely have sought him out, after all she had said herself that she had been following him since time immemorial.

Angela with her ritual had unlocked infinite possibilities for him to grow, now it was up to him to make them bloom, to contain more knowledge he had to modify the "container", this container was his mind. In this incarnation he knew that his mind was the key to expanding his soul.

He could start from a very good base as he mastered thought control and presence in the Here and Now, nothing in his life's past influenced him in a negative way. From the past he only processed the lessons provided by experience and nothing from the future disturbed him, he was with the mind in the present, since it is in the present that you build the future you want.

Without the old prejudices and fears, he could assimilate the Secrets of the great alchemists of the past, and apply the rituals giving them the importance they deserved.

On a rainy evening, sitting at home in front of the fireplace, he drew up on a notepad the program that

according to him had to be implemented, summarizing it in 3 points, to be carried out in ascending order:

1) Economic independence

This kind of studies needed a lot of time, he could no longer work 8 hours a day.

2) Money to travel

Surely advanced masters who could have helped him and libraries where important instructions could be found, surely he would not have found them under the house. He had to earn good money.

3) Unshakable faith in spiritual growth.

He had to make the most of this life he was living, the goal was the immortality of the soul, so as not to lose any of the acquired teachings. Had he not succeeded, the rebirth would have formatted everything, and the gap between the two would have widened further.

He decided that the legendary Philosopher's Stone of the Alchemists was the goal. He began immediately the next day, without delay. He got into his car, drove to work as he had done for years at that part of the job and... He went to hand in his letter of resignation, there was general dismay throughout the office, it was insane to leave a safe and well-paid job.

One of his best friends and colleagues pulled him aside.

"David tell me, have you found anything better? Why are you leaving this quiet, well-paid job? You know that others would make fake cards to stay in your place."

David held him close and reassured him, "Don't worry, everything's under control in a few weeks. I'm starting my new job."

David said goodbye to everyone, with many now had almost a fraternal relationship and stayed in their embraces for a long time.

When he left the place where he had spent years of his life, he turned back and looked at that structure but immediately came to his senses, manifestations of nostalgia he could not afford, he immediately converted them into emotions of gratitude for everything he had learned from that work and from those magnificent people.

Now came the good part, he had to find a job that would give him the freedom and money he needed, and he didn't even know where to start.

He had a little hoard that he had saved up over the years, and the payoff he had to cash in. He could invest in a business, perhaps to run online, that would give him the money and the freedom he needed.

He spent days and nights carefully researching how best to invest, with his mind at full capacity. He was 100% focused on what to do. After all the analysis he thought it was appropriate to do, he decided to invest in the electronics industry. Marketing this type of products so widely in demand on the market could prove to be the winning move. After having carefully chosen an Asian retailer through the internet and after a long negotiation, he issued the first order of electronic material chosen personally from the lists that had been sent to him. He had spent well, placing a large order and negotiating a good price. He was sure to make good sales.

After a few days the material arrived as agreed, and he began to use the online sales platforms to offer the items he had purchased.

It was immediately a success! He sold everything quickly, with earnings that exceeded his expectations.

He was amazed to note that if he committed himself positively, remaining focused only on the present moment, he could get results at the first attempt, why hadn't he thought of it before? Simple, he was too anchored to his comfort zone and the given security of fixed work. Before Angela's ritual, the mere thought of trying something like this would have terrified him.

He went straight to the tax authorities, setting up an individual company. After a few months the turnover was considerable, he had to hire two employees to manage sales and rent a storage warehouse for goods arriving from suppliers. He was satisfied, he had achieved the first point on the list in times he had not even remotely expected.

It was time to organize his new business so that it would take off on its own and free him from the need to always be present to manage the business.

She had chosen two trusted collaborators, two young people who married and loved David's project from the first moment. They showed from the beginning that they knew how to manage business from the heart, and after a period of working

alongside them during which he trained
them at work, he understood that the time
had come to do it on their own.

The right people are in the right places.

It had been quite some time since David had been alone on the phone with his two co-workers. Business was booming, and all he could do was pick up the profits and give sporadic directions.

It was clear, he had also made the second point of the list, he could now become financially independent.

The time had come for him to study and realize point three of the list, hard work on himself for spiritual growth, he had to grow if he wanted to see her again. He began a journey throughout Europe in search of the best esoteric bookshops. He studied rare and ancient volumes, he consulted some of them also from private collections, but after a few months of research he still had not identified the right path to take. After various researches and thousands of kilometers travelled, he decided to go to London after having taken some information about a well-stocked esoteric library, where he could find ancient and interesting texts on how to master the Energy and how to obtain the famous "Philosopher's Stone" of the alchemists, the immortality of the soul , to avoid that with physical death he would start all over again.

He arrived on a cold March morning in the big city. He settled down in the apartment he had rented online and after resting for a few hours, he threw himself into the tangled jungle of London. After quite a few difficulties, slightly outside the city, he found the library he was looking for, a very old place with many bookshelves, some of which could only be reached by stairs. There were a few visitors scattered here and

there consulting books, all assorted in reading. David went without wasting time in the area of his interest, dedicated to the writings of spirituality and esotericism. There was a book already on the counter that had not been put away in his dedicated accommodation, he thought he'd put it back in its place and concentrate on finding the lyrics he was interested in, when he took a look at the cover before putting it back. It was the Alphabet of Ben Sira, a book of cabalistic philosophy. The Kabbalah was not the main object of his studies at the time, but he decided to open it and take a look anyway.

He took a page at random and his attention was captured by part of the text:

"She said, I will not stand beneath you. And he said, and I will not lie beneath you, but only above you. It is suitable for you to lie only below, whereas I am made to lie above."

The writing referred to the story of Lilith, who in many ancient Hebrew texts like that was depicted as the original wife of Adam, the first man. David knew the story broadly, Lilith was initially created as Adam, and not by a rib like Eve. But Adam wanted her as his servant and submissive. She fled from Eden enraged with

God, and according to tradition, began to live among demons. With the flight from Eden she kept her nature of being immortal because she did not commit original sin by eating from the tree forbidden by God. From her figure were born various legends, among which that of being the first of all witches.

He closed the volume to store it, and suddenly a scent of orange blossom reached him.

"It's you, Angela!"

He exclaimed, turning in every direction, hoping to find her nearby. He saw no female person around him.

At one point he was like struck by lightning.

"The dream!" He cried out loud, turning the few present in his direction. He told them a dream he had

during his holiday on the Amalfi Coast. He remembered very well that eastern scenery of the dream, and Angela in the temple. When she asked him who she was, she told him to look for her name in the Kabbalah.

A shiver down his spine attacked him. He couldn't believe it, but at the same time he thought it couldn't be a coincidence. He had met, dated and... made love with the legendary Lilith, perhaps one of the most powerful beings who had ever walked the Earth. The circle was closing at that precise moment, in conjunction with the closing of that book closed. Even the scroll of the ritual that allowed him to gain liberation from limiting thought patterns and control over emotions... She had written it.

While he was still there, with the book in his hand and grainy eyes staring into the void, a voice brought him back to reality.

"Sir, are you all right? Are you all right?"

David came to his senses and turned to see who he was talking to. He was a distinguished person, elegantly dressed. He was about fifty or so.

"I saw you making an exclamation in what I think was Italian, and then you looked terrified. Is everything all right?"

The man continued with a smile.

"Yes yes, it's all right," replied David in a rather do-it-yourself English, "while reading a little piece of this book I smelled the same perfume that someone I know always wears and I thought she was here, no big deal.

"The Alphabet of Ben Sira" said the man looking at the book,

"are you interested in Kabbalistic Philosophy?" The man asked again.

"No, I was looking for some volume of alchemy, I'm very interested in obtaining the Philosopher's Stone.

This text had been left by someone on the desk and I just wanted to put it back in its place. But before I could not avoid to browse inside. "

The man looked at David and smiled, then spoke again.

"Be careful when you feel like opening a book on a random page, it means there might be an important

message for you. I always do it with the Bible!"

David smiled at him. He was an interesting person.

"I'm Anthony Miller, and if you'd like to have a chat, we could have tea together."

David gladly accepted. He was the first person who had invited him to speak a little since he had decided to embark on that journey for personal growth. On his path, he left behind only busy souls, and people focused on their business.

The two stopped at a bar and began to talk at length, before their lives, and in the end, about what had pushed them into that very special bookstore. Anthony explained to David that he was there for some texts about astral travel, English had been seriously involved in this kind of practice for almost two years, but until

then it had never been successful. According to those who have managed to acquire this ability, you can travel through all universes and see incredible places and civilizations; this fascinated him but so far he had only managed to achieve a series of what insiders call "conscious dreams", many times he was able to be

aware of dreaming, and be an active part, but the trip was something else entirely. David interrupted him.

"What practices are you using? I've never been into it, but I can give you some advice on that. I've read about it, maybe it can help you."

Anthony was very happy to exchange a few opinions with that sunny, smiling Italian. Finding an interlocutor who was interested in these topics was always rare.

"I'm trying the repetition technique. With repetitive sentences that contain the intent of the journey, I bring

myself to the point of waking sleep, seeking the detachment of the astral body."

David, after listening carefully, suggested it.

"I read about people who could successfully make astral journeys after reaching a high point of relaxation, then visualizing a figure similar to themselves outside the body and imagining transferring the five senses into it. By practicing daily and taking more and more control over the astral alter ego, they claimed to be able,

from a certain moment on, to achieve the famous detachment".

He felt to add that in any case, it was in him, before deepening the techniques and succeeding concretely in astral travel, he would devote himself to a training course to obtain a good "centering" of his Being, indispensable to obtain control of emotions and manage the possible fears arising from what can be seen in

that kind of experience.

Anthony pulled out of a pocket of the elegant vest wearing a small notebook, on which he meticulously reported all the information received. As soon as he finished his transcriptions, he took a sip of tea and asked David what kind of book he was looking for in that place.

"I was looking for a text with valid notions for the production of the legendary 'Philosopher's Stone', the ultimate material produced by the alchemists."

The Englishman looked at him smiling

"if by any chance you can turn vile metal into gold... Remember me!"

Even David laughed. He explained to Anthony that it was not the property of transforming lead into gold possessed by the famous Stone that he was looking for, but it was the correct way to obtain the Philosopher's Stone to which he aspired. This gave the Alchemist the Body of the Immortal Soul, which

would allow him to constantly learn the secrets of the Universe without the interference of the cycle of death and rebirth.

"You seem to have a real knack for this, even though you are, at first glance, a little over thirty."

Anthony told him impressed. "I have a manual that might come in handy. It's all about alchemy. I bought it at a street market. It seemed ancient and interesting, so I bought it thinking of reading it one day, but my passions now as then were

others, and they never allowed me to start it. I can give the book to you without any problem."

David suddenly had a flashback, he was reminded of a conference he attended some time ago, where the theme was The Resonance Law. The lecturer explained that in the Universe we attract to us what vibrates at the frequency of our energy field. Our thoughts and emotions influence our energy field, so who we meet on

our path, and what will happen to us, will be the derivative that we consciously or unconsciously established ourselves. Favorable encounters like in this case, that kind and helpful Englishman, or the success of his feat of economic independence were the result of the control he was able to have over his mind thanks to Lilith's ritual. Thanks to the fall of his constituted ego, with all his fears and prejudices, he

was always able to polarize his mind on thoughts full of positivity, and the Universe responded positively to referrals.

"David all right? Are you there?"

Anthony brought him back to earth.

"Sure, I'd love to take a look at the volume!"

David responded enthusiastically.

The Great Opera

David decided not to return to the bookstore, he wanted to analyze first the book he had been promised without wasting any more energy. He thought that if that meeting had happened, with good probability, it had to be the lead to follow. The two met again several times in the following days, and as promised, during a walk the Englishman gave him the text of Alchemy.

"Here's the book, I hope it's of use to you. I confess I only opened it to give you a peek at the introduction, so I couldn't tell you anything about its contents."

David turned it over in his hands, the volume was quite big, and judging by its appearance it seemed to date back at least to the early twentieth century, the author signed himself as "Antoine Dumas", as soon as he read the writer's name he had a little plunge to his heart, but he could not explain why, since he had never

read it in any text before.

He thanked him warmly for the gift, and in return he invited Anthony for a vacation in Italy as soon as he wanted. Before saying goodbye, David told him:

"Each of us crosses the path of another human being for a reason, to give or to have; whether it be things or teachings. May I soon be as useful to you as you were to me."

"You've already given me so much and you don't know it. Your advice, your passion, the fire in your eyes burning for the

Extraordinary. Knowing that people like you still exist is already a great gift to me." Anthony answered.

The two hugged and said goodbye; they both knew they would always look for each other, from that meeting a wonderful bond was born between them. David went to the apartment he had in a short rent, got in touch with the landlord to see if he could keep it for another week. There were no problems.

He decided to study Anthony's book for a week, and see if it might be useful to him, or he would inevitably have to go and look for some more reading material in the library as well as from initial plans.

When he was studying, he didn't want to be disturbed. He did not drink alcohol or eat meat, as prescribed by the procedures.

Before starting from the beginning of the book, he analyzed it in its various parts, to see if it was what he expected, and the expectations were those of a text with effective rituals to perform. He

didn't need the usual manuals that talked about theory, he wanted something rare, other than the usual texts. After an initial analysis he was satisfied, most likely he was in the presence of very precious material.

The book, written by a self-styled alchemist, really contained unpublished information that he had never read or heard before. It was articulated by a first part made of terminologies and theoretical explanations, a second part dedicated to the equipment for the laboratory where the alchemist was to carry out his

training, and a third part composed of rituals that would work both on matter and in the spiritual sphere.

This is because, as the book itself reported at the beginning of the third part:

"the ability to modify matter had to go hand in hand with the practitioner's inner growth."

After dealing with the first part of the volume, he realized that he could not finish the reading there in England. He would need his house, or rather his garage, to build the workshop, and set it up with the

equipment for the exercises shown in the book.

He worked hard to find the first flight leaving for Italy, and before leaving he decided to stop by and say goodbye to Anthony; it was all thanks to him that he had been able to find a complete and detailed volume so quickly, and that allowed, at least from the premises, to move from words to deeds.

David found him at home, the Englishman was all absorbed in a project he was developing. In life he was a successful engineer. Anthony promised to visit him as soon as possible with great pleasure. He had been to Italy several times, and would gladly come back again.

David left him with the promise that by the time Anthony decided to visit him, he would be well on his way.

As soon as he returned, David immediately set to work setting up his garage as reported in the old alchemist's book. He got rid of everything that was taking up space, and started getting the material. Many things, such as stills for distillation and stoves he was able to find easily, for others, such as special herbs or crucibles to melt metals was a bit more complicated. After a few weeks, he was finally able to observe his finished work. That garage was now a perfect alchemical laboratory as described in the book.

What David liked about that text was that he didn't need masters to monitor the practitioner's work.

He didn't need to go looking for a complete alchemist to help him. The book had a process of self-control, of growth with experiments at the end of each lesson, if the result of those experiments was as described in the book, it meant that the lesson had been assimilated by the apprentice.

"Many great men of Knowledge have tried to make the Ancient Knowledge available to all," David thought,

"Unfortunately, the skepticism that has been instilled in mankind by the Dark Powers has never allowed the

greatest possible number of individuals to make the evolutionary leap, they have always preferred us so, to go gallivanting in our ignorance."

Days went by, and David was totally absorbed in that volume. He "felt" within himself the correctness of that information, and he performed the exercises with the utmost zeal, leaving nothing out, not even the smallest detail.

He was able in a short time to produce various curative distillates, which synthesized active ingredients of natural plants. Distillates that substituted medicines in all respects. Parallel to the work he did on the matter, he developed the alchemical-spiritual path that derived from those distillates. It was not only the effect of the active ingredient of the preparation that worked, but the Loving Power that he impressed during the distillation phase that made everything effective.

"Everything on this Earth, refined and worked in the right way, brings to light its highest quality." He watched.

David wrote down all his progress in a diary, and when he read it again he thought about the work of the ancient shamans. Great Souls like the Don Juan of Castaneda's books acted in the matter because they were not contaminated by any power of the "modern world. For this reason, they already knew everything that

he was now making commitment to study, since they were not involved in the corruption of matter, the contact with the entity that Lilith called GIEM was almost direct.

"How nice it would be to meet you now, I would like to show you all the progress I am making. I'm sure she'd be proud of me."

He thought in his mind, as the moments where those green eyes hypnotized him

against the background of the paradise of the Amalfi Coast flowed before his eyes.

After a day consisting of several hours of study of the text and various experiments, he wanted to take advantage of his fatigue to try the exercise of astral travel that he suggested to Anthony, and maybe try the strong centering he had matured in recent times.

"When you're tired, it should be much easier to go to sleep."

He thought.

After achieving a deep state of drowsiness, he began the procedure of visualization of

the astral body, the transfer of the senses...
And, he did not believe it. He succeeded at
the first attempt! He floated lightly in the
air in his room with his astral body, he
could go anywhere in the universe he
wanted.

Englishman was right, it was a fantastic
experience to try. But now, what to do in
that condition? He thought of the desire
he had expressed a moment before; to
meet that extraordinary entity again. That
temple where he met Lilith a

few years ago in a dream... He could have
tried to reach that place, and who knows,
maybe meet her there.

Perhaps she had changed her mind,
perhaps after some time she would have
agreed to reconnect with him.

The "teleportation" bore fruit, after a few
seconds he was outside that temple again,
in that same Middle Eastern place of

another era. This time, however, he was amazed. Outside the building he saw Anthony, very elegant in his twentieth century attire.

"Anthony, what are you doing here?"

The Englishman looked at him with an air of satisfaction.

"Aren't you going to congratulate me for hooking you up?"

He answered slyly.

Since they'd split up in London, Anthony must have developed some advanced astral travel skills.

"I congratulate you, dear friend. But my question is... How the hell did you get into my astral travel?"

David replied in amazement.

"Have you ever heard of quantum entanglement? When two or more particles come into contact and develop affinities by interacting for a given period of time, even when they separate they remain linked on a vibrational level, and space and time do not separate them. Using recently learned techniques that exploit

these principles of quantum physics, while I was on one of my trips I "heard" you and intercepted you, and so...

Here I am! But since when have you become interested in astral travel?"

Anthony replied, intrigued.

David, out of delicacy, did not want to tell him the truth, that he had succeeded quite easily at the first blow. He knew that Anthony had studied those practices for quite a while, collecting long periods of failure.

"For some time now, along with the alchemy studies that I'm primarily interested in, I've been supporting this kind of research." He answered.

The Englishman looked at him puzzled.

"I've decided to get involved in this absurd situation, in the middle of who knows what era, what are we doing here?"

"I wanted to go to that temple, and if I'm lucky, I should find Lilith, the First Woman, inside it.

"For the first time since she met him, David read an expression of terror on his friend's face.

"I don't know the exact level of your knowledge, but if you're not some very powerful Wizard of the Order,

you're definitely a fool to look for an entity like this. I think you know that Lilith, along with Adam is one of the two First Beings, didn't eat the apple of sin and for this reason she never lost her immortality.

The ancient Hebrew texts narrate that after her escape from Eden she always lived with the worst demons,

without detracting from the fact that legends want her as the founder of all witches.

David didn't get out of the way.

"I should know what I'm doing." He answered him.

"Go ahead, I'll wait for you here as soon as you finish. I have no intention of going in there." The Englishman left his blessing, taking advantage of that unexpected journey to explore that strange place, while waiting for his friend.

David was about to cross the threshold of the ancient structure, moving his first steps inside, he was able to observe the identical scenario of the previous dream, a room crowded with followers, and the throne elevated. Sitting on the throne was she, as beautiful as ever, wrapped in a gorgeous long silk dress of the same color as her eyes. As soon as she saw him, she got up from her seat and walked towards him, with the stride of her long legs it seemed to take a moment to reach him. It may have been an astral voyage, but when she was near him David could smell the intoxicating scent that emanated.

"You understood who I am from the Kabbalah, as I told you. As an enthusiast, you should know a lot about me. I congratulate you on your daring, I told you we should never see each other again and you even dared in astral to look for me."

David wanted to answer but she didn't give him the time.

"In any case, you deserved my esteem, because you had the courage to follow the path I indicated to unlock your talents, and this is not for everyone. You human beings have free will, and the freedom to manage it, and very often you do it wrong. I can only open a path to those who have potential, then it is up to those

who have been chosen to take it. I reiterate my joy to see that you followed my suggestions, but as I told you the last time we met, you don't have to look for me anymore, my action towards you must be limited to

what we shared. When your soul is big enough, and if I ever feel it, I will manifest myself to you. This is the last time I warn you, or you will be lost."

David listened to every word, and despite all the stability that came from the ritual she had given him, being in his presence was very demanding.

But he liked that, she was the impossible challenge for which he would not take a single step back.

"I wish I had the chance to see you again in the time I'm living so I could spend it with you. You have almost unlimited power, I know this and I respect it, and throughout all the millennia you have gone through,

surely many humans have hoped to get into your good graces to get this or that. And I also know that you could destroy me in a second, but I have no interest in getting anything from you except your presence.

If I'm pursuing the Power now, it's only to get to you." He answered her.

Lilith looked at him with a smile.

"Yours is a very dangerous game, I choose who can run by my side and can learn from my lips. But running to my side and learning from my lips is not for everyone. I hope you understand that."

The mighty entity took a second of silence, noticed with pleasure that he did not lower his gaze, there was no reverential fear in his eyes.

He continued, "Get the Philosopher's Stone for which you are working, only with the Body of the Immortal Soul that comes from it will I be able to be close to you. But it's not so easy.

When you get it, you'll have to create the ritual to invoke me yourself. It has to be a powerful ritual that will have to prove your Immortal

Soul to me, and in which you will have total faith in what you are doing. These are great things that I'm asking of you. The ritual will require you to put everything into play, if you fail, you will lose this life with everything you have learned. The choice is yours, you can refuse now and continue to live your quiet life without ever looking for me again. Until then, I will not reveal myself."

David saw her turn back and return to her throne, then suddenly darkness. The alarm clock... He was in his bed and it was morning.

The true Master makes you Master of
yourself

David stayed there in his bed for a few minutes reflecting on what happened before he got up. He thought about all the spiritual path he had taken to get to her, the time had come for the final rush. He had to gather all his strength to complete his path and acquire enough knowledge to carry out the ritual that she had

expected, now he had finally had a chance.

"Sooner or later, everyone discovers their own goal to fight for in life. The price I should pay is the price I will pay."

He thought with confidence.

After he got up, he took his Smartphone and there were several messages from Anthony, asking him to call as soon as possible. David was strangely exhausted after that troubled night, decided to have breakfast, and only then he called.

The two said goodbye, then David opened the argument from the night before.

"Anthony, what happened to you on the astral flight?"

"what happened to you," replied the clearly irritated Englishman, "do you realize that I waited a lifetime outside that temple? I've been worried so far, knowing what kind of entity you'd find in front of."

David justified himself by explaining how things had gone.

"I didn't abandon you at all, after I finished talking to Lilith, she turned her back on me and I think she somehow brought down my astral travel."

The Englishman could not yet believe that he had met a person who had the ability to come into contact

with an entity like Lilith without suffering consequences.

"If I'm not indiscreet, how come you're trying to get in touch with this kind of being?"

"It's very intimate. It touches me personally. I'm sorry, but I don't feel like telling you any more for the moment."

It was Anthony who immediately apologized. From the tone of voice he understood that David must have been really taken by that story and decided to change the subject; but before doing so, he advised him to be very careful.

"Well, now that you've learned about astral travel, and if you want to meet there, it certainly won't be a good excuse not to visit you physically. If you're available, I've decided to visit you next month. Get off your schedule because I want you to take me to some nice places!"

David was enthusiastic about it, he needed to get away from the studies that absorbed him almost all day and take a break. He thought that a little distraction with a good friend could only help his concentration.

Getting in touch with Lilith was what he wanted most, but it wasn't an obsession that would undo him. Life offered many forms of love to cultivate, including friendship.

During the period leading up to Anthony's arrival, David decided to make the most of his time by starting to study the last paragraph of the book, he had a month to finish it, and perhaps he could make it.

"The control of matter through speech."

It was the title, "the most interesting part so far," he thought.

He threw himself headlong into the first theoretical part, which explained in depth how to give power to the

spoken words and influence events; after a careful study that lasted a week, he began the first experiments suggested by the volume. In the first exercise he had to mix powder of different natural colors in a transparent container full of water and prevent them from mixing. It took several days before he could "tune in" the material he was working with; the work involved feeling each molecule of the water and the colored powder in the glass as his own molecule, once he had empathized with the action he was carrying out, as reported in the theory, he began to transmit the Power with faith in the words of the ritual he had performed for the occasion. Here at last the powder was compacted into strips in the water inside the glass, just as he had mentally visualized it.

His heart overflowed with joy, it was his first small "miracle", a manipulation of matter in every respect.

"This experiment reflects what great artists do in their art, in fact art is a real form of magic in front of everyone's eyes, but no one notices it", he thought of those who take wonderful paintings out of a canvas and colors, or those who with a chisel and a hammer transform an inexpressive block of marble into a breathtaking work.

"Most men draw on the Power that the Universe makes available to them in a totally unconscious way to turn thoughts into reality. There is no limit to what could be done if we were all aware of it. The difference between the common man and the alchemist lies in the fact that the alchemist studies to implement this

Power with awareness, as I have done today". He concluded.

He had a few more days left before Anthony's arrival, and decided to stay with the studio so he had time to arrange a nice stay for his friend.

Where could he take him? Anthony once told him that he had already been to Italy, to cities like Rome, Milan and Florence. He immediately thought of the Amalfi Coast, it was the ideal place to show the English, and it was also the perfect place to perform the Last Ritual, the one that should guarantee him access to the

Body of the Immortal Soul. Which location was more suitable than the one where he first met that 's

seemingly harmless and charming redheaded girl who turned out to be the First Woman.

She had rented the house that would host them for a few weeks on the Coast and the itinerary they would do had already been planned; now all that remained was to go to pick Anthony up at the airport.

The two friends finally met on the physical plane this time, after a long time. After saying goodbye at the airport exit, they got in the car and David immediately asked him about his studies.

The Englishman explained to him that in his research he had managed to get in touch with an Indian expert in this practice, and that after being followed by the latter in the exercises, he had managed to achieve significant improvements in a very short time, until he mastered the practice in an excellent way.

"And anyway, my dear friend, your cue was crucial."

Anthony said referring to the suggestion David gave him about astral travel the day they met;

"in practice my Master encouraged me to persevere on that path, the effectiveness of this method was also supported by him. If I can give you some advice, look for someone further ahead of you in the practices you want to acquire, and ask for his support. The help of a good Master increases growth significantly more

than self-learning."

"It's the masters I wanted to talk to you about."

Said David, looking for the right words to express himself.

"I assume you're free to believe me or not, and if you think I'm crazy I'll understand if you want me to drive you back to the airport; remember when you asked me about Lilith, and why I wanted to get in touch with her?"

"Of course I remember." Anthony answered with interest.

"Lilith is a kind of teacher to me, or rather, that's what I'd like. She manifested herself at a time in my life, precisely during that famous vacation on the Coast I took a few years ago. With a powerful ritual she freed me from the negative influence of my ego, thus intervening on many factors that limited my ability to learn, such as negative emotions about myself and others".

David told him the whole story of his meeting with Lilith, by now he felt he could trust that always positive man who, like him, shared an interest in the Extraordinary.

Anthony listened to everything in silence without intervening even once. When David was finished, he was literally speechless. It took him a few minutes to work out what he thought of the story.

"Take me back to the airport!" Anthony said inexpressively.

After a few seconds, however, he burst out laughing, David put his hand on his forehead and begged him to be serious. After his usual irony he recovered his seriousness and congratulated him. He gave him his thoughts,

"my friend, you must be a sort of favorite entered into her good graces, a Monad that she has been following for several eons already, and that she has decided to help personally. She wants to help you, but she knows very well that she must contain her intervention: to be in contact with a being of infinite knowledge as she could lead to madness a human being who does not have the right degree of growth, and so get lost forever. If you've sought her out without her consent and she hasn't destroyed you, you can see that she cares for you."

That concludes Anthony.

"Here's the thing, Lilith didn't destroy me on that night I went to her on astral, but she might if I fail the ritual."

"Explain yourself." English retorted again.

David confided to him what Lilith said to himself that night in the temple, and what ritual he had to perform to demonstrate the attainment of the Immortal Soul if he wanted to see her again.

"I personally would go there with cold feet, this game is a risk in which I would not take part. I would have accepted the growth aid graciously provided and honestly would have sought someone else to learn the Way. But it is also true that each of us has our own path, and I don't want to influence or judge yours, so my

advice is that you must listen to your Heart, if it tells you that you have the skills to stand this test, then do so. But take care to be true to yourself, listen only to your heart, no whispering of the mind should intrude".

But I've already decided," replied David, "it's a valuable opportunity and I intend to take it. I could not conclude this incarnation in the total absence of her, so in doing so, I would be aware of throwing something that is too valuable to me."

Anthony shook his head left and right, called him crazy and... asked him to take him out to eat. He was hungry.

After dinner at a nice farmhouse with game and good local wine, they went home. David proudly showed all the work he had done to fulfill the "alchemist's requirements" imposed by the volume Anthony had given him, and illustrated all the results achieved.

"Boy, did you manage to achieve this degree of knowledge all by yourself, without anyone's help? I'm amazed!"

David looked at him gloating.

"It's all thanks to your book, really well written. I did it all by myself, but it's as if I've been joined by a Grand Master."

"Who the hell wrote that?"

Anthony still said with amazement on his face.

"Actually, that's what I wanted to ask you." answered David,

"I searched everywhere for information about the author, a certain Antoine Dumas, but I found nothing, not even information about the publishing house of the work. Most likely, no information about the press has been entered at his request."

"Antoine Dumas... Never heard of him." Anthony confirmed it.

The two friends remained for quite a while in their discussions when they realized that it was already two o'clock in the morning, and they were due to leave the next morning.

Bet everything on the coin falling down

After breakfast, early in the morning the two friends were already on their way to the Amalfi Coast. The succession of Italian landscapes left the Englishman astonished. Italy could boast a truly incredible landscape heritage. The program illustrated by David was very appealing to Anthony, a few weeks of sea and

sunshine would not only benefit his heart but also his health. After a few hours of travel, they had arrived at their destination. They went to the address where the house for rent was located and, to their surprise, they found no one there waiting for them. The door was closed and no one answered the phone or intercom. David immediately took his Smartphone out of his pocket to look for more information about the platform where he had found the property, but only then he noticed an e-mail from the landlord, who had cancelled the rental period for personal reasons and issued a refund. Taken from all his things he had not noticed.

"Now what do we do?" Anthony asked him.

"We'll find another place, don't worry." David reassured him. They went around a lot looking for apartments in that area but nothing, in the end they landed in a hotel and asked for availability.

"We're all booked up, there's a reservation that hasn't been paid yet, but I can't cancel."

The girl at the reception answered seriously and impassively.

David intervened in an intense tone of voice, looking her in the eyes, "can't we make an exception? For six

days I will now pay the amount due."

He kept looking at her, the girl looked at him and answered after a few seconds, "ok we'll make an exception", she answered almost like an automaton.

After the payment they went to the room and deposited their things.

"What happened down there with the girl at reception?" Anthony asked curious. "I've been watching the scene, and I think you've done some sort of manipulation, or spell. She was so convinced not to give us the room because of the rules, then all of a sudden she changed her mind after you asked her."

David replied with a goliardic smile,

"You shouldn't do such things, but since I read in her voice an extreme application of the rules, when she could very well turn a blind eye, I persuaded her by impressing Power in my words and looking eyes in the eyes."

"You are dangerous son, don't ever look me in the eyes again!" said Anthony smiling, "and you don't do those things anyway. Have you been able to do this for a long time?"

"This is a talent I developed with the last paragraph of your book, which teaches just how to give power to words and look to change matter. In any case I have never used esoteric knowledge in my life to manipulate people or events with the awareness of creating problems. These are practices that affect black magic, of

this field I am not interested."

Glad to hear that, don't ever change from the light to the dark side, remember that."

"I'll always keep that in mind." David answered.

He quickly spent a week of total immersion in the splendor of the Amalfi Coast, between relaxing days of

swimming in the sea and magical evenings spent in the music of the various kiosks, under a starry sky to take your breath away. The last evening had already arrived, and the two friends were in front of a bar sipping a drink; David broke the silence.

"I should ask you a favor."

"How can I help you?" Anthony replied, noting the great seriousness on his face.

"This is the last night we are here, and I have prepared the ritual, my proof of the Immortal Soul. What I ask is that you take the car and accompany me before midnight where I will show you, then you must leave me there and go. If I'm not back by morning, you can leave without me. The car is rented, you can return it

safely at the airport, and return to England; as soon as possible I'll be in touch".

There were a few minutes of silence, Anthony understood, and without saying anything he nodded his head.

Just before midnight the two were at David's chosen place, it was the place where he made love with Lilith the last time they saw each other on the Coast;

they both got out of the car and hugged each other tightly.

"This is not goodbye," David said, holding him even harder. "I know, but unfortunately I haven't met any witch on duty who has performed some kind of ritual on me on Control, I can't help but suffer the possibility of a friend leaving this life."

"You think everything's going to be all right, now I have to go."

Gently David let go, Anthony did the same. He got in his car and drove off in the dark of night.

David, left alone, began to put into practice the plan he had planned for the ritual, he had planned everything in the smallest possible way.

He set out to climb a small road that led to an elevated point of the harbor. Up it, could observe the sea as black as night, with on the background a huge full moon that gave poetry to the landscape, difficult to describe. Up there many professionals and stuntmen would often do diving breathtaking practice that left passers-by astonished; to the eyes and cross the jump was about a hundred feet and he hadn't even jumped from a six-foot trampoline in his life. He could see in the distance the rocks where met Lilith that last night. He began to prepare, it was the time to put everything he had to good use without doubt and hesitation. Displayed with the mind he thought about what was going to happen and prepared himself with the maximum concentration in pronouncing the evocation with the words of power that he had developed to transfer his awareness in the Body of the Immortal Soul, the one which is considered one of the last pieces of evidence were subjected to the alchemists of the past. In this ritual, any fear of death had to be reset to zero with the total certainty of "feeling" your Body Immortal compound of Upper Matter accumulated in the path he had travelled up to that point, and that would have hosted his self forever, even after the death.

He took off all his clothes, remained totally naked and led to the edge of the cliff. The heart was calm, the projection of his Immortal Body was fixed in his mind and his faith was total. Now he could proceed, uttered the ritual words and threw himself into the void assuming the position of the diver with his arms outstretched over his head and the hands joined. That descent of a few seconds didn't seem ever end up suddenly having the most violent impact with the sea and then... Just darkness and silence.

"David, pull yourself together." Suddenly
a female voice, at first in distance, then
closer and closer.

 David, pull yourself together. I'm here."

Suddenly the senses were coming back,
that's the sound of the waves around his
head, the cold sea water, night of early
summer, the light of that enchanting
moon

... full of reflections on the sea... He was
alive!

He turned quickly around, who had
spoken to him?

He recognized her immediately, it was
she, Lilith, who was swimming... quietly
lying supine in the water, enjoying the sky
quilt of stars.

"Don't you think there's too much beauty
being ignored? A night-time bathing costs
nothing but generates emotions in those

who knows how to grasp to make you the happiest creature in the world.

And when we grasp the beauty of creation, GIEM also draws from it... enjoyment."

He saw her and burst into tears like a baby. He cried of a primordial joy, that joy that must not have explanations. He simply had the heart that was exploding with joy for her.

He swam quickly to meet her, grabbed her and gave her a long, intense kiss that tasted like salt. Despite the aroma of the sea, he could smell the scent of orange blossom that she was using, it was a drug for him.

Then she hugged him tight, they stayed so long, caressing his head while the tears of joy still slipped on the cheeks.

She invited him to swim to shore, where she had prepared a duffel bag with towels and bathrobes. David went to get a towel, but she stopped him.

"Antoine Dumas, the author of the book that led you here...it was you. It was you who wrote it; in your own previous reincarnation you were an alchemist of end eight hundred. At that time you failed the final test in your path, do you want to know why?"

David, a little shaky in the fresh night sea air... nodded.

"The teachings I pointed out to you for your growth found a wall of selfishness in your heart. Yours interest in me was, albeit in a small part, contaminated by interest in material goods. You wanted using me for power. You were like all the other alchemists and then they failed. But this time it was different. Interest in me was sincere and I allowed you to access the Knowledge."

"How did you know for sure that this time, too... we're not selfish ends?" He answered.

"Nothing could be clearer. In your previous incarnation, your heart did not achieve sufficient purity, and this didn't allow you blind faith and total indispensable love... to complete the Last Trial you completed a little while ago, and simply died in the ritual."

The moonlight illuminated her, she was still naked, and beautiful like a goddess. David didn't care anymore, he was there in front of her, and they were immersed in what might have been heaven on earth. They stayed there that night, asleep- hugging each other on the beach.

Anthony now back in the English metropolis, had resumed his activities.

Between one project and another, his thoughts flew constantly to David. What was the outcome of the test? Was he okay? Out of respect of his friend's will, had resisted until that moment to the temptation to call, or to write a message; but He felt he couldn't take it anymore, he had an unbearable wizard.

He picked up the phone and dialed the number, the automatic voice... told him the number was nonexistent.

He immediately thought the worst, he'd take the first one flight available to Italy to make sure it was at the sure. Suddenly, someone knocked on the door.

Anthony swooped in the hope that it was the friend who had come there for a surprised but he opened up and found himself in front of the postman. It was a package for him, had been sent from an anonymous center shipments.

Without delay he quickly opened the package, inside was the book she gave David, and a note that said...

"We'll see each other again, in this life or another. This I wrote it, and now I'm giving it to you when you want to read it, it will come in handy."

Anthony cried and understood.

"We'll see each other again. I'll be waiting for you."

He said it in his heart.

Every character mentioned in this book

and every situation is the result of inventiveness

of the writer.

Cover picture:

"The woman reader" Federico Faruffini 1865 - Oil on canvas

Exhibited at the Modern Art Gallery in Milan

www.ingramcontent.com/pod-product-compliance
Lightning Source LLC
Chambersburg PA
CBHW021218130726
47988CB00002B/704